MEDICI BOOKS FOR CHILDREN

Biddy Finds a Hare

by Audrey Tarrant

 Code 85503027 5

Biddy, the beagle puppy, was bored. She wanted to go for a walk, but John, her young master, was still at school. It was a long time to wait until he came home.

Her mother had once told her what fun it was to chase a hare.
If only she could chase a hare now!
A butterfly fluttered past her nose, into
the flowerbed and through a hole in the fence.

She sniffed the hole and then began to dig hard with her front paws.
A thrush watched from a branch and scolded her.
Soon the hole would be deep enough for
her to squeeze through, and she could follow the butterfly.

At last the hole was big enough, and she was in the field. She ran along
with nose down, smelling the buttercups and clover.
She was not looking where she was going,
and nearly bumped into the baby donkey, lying in the field.

Which way should she go to find a hare? "Buzz-buzz-buzz", said a bumble bee in her ear, and then it flew off towards the orchard. Biddy followed it across the field and under the fence.

Biddy went to one of the lambs under the apple tree, and barked "Hello" to him. The lamb was so surprised he jumped into the air and then ran bleating to his mother.

Plodding on through the orchard, Biddy heard loud chirpings. She looked up into the apple tree, and saw a family of bluetits. Sitting down, she watched while the mother tit fed her babies with flies.

When the tits flew away into a field, Biddy followed them.

There she saw a calf with its mother. "I will bark at the calf and make her jump like the lamb", thought Biddy. But when she was near the calf, the cow mooed loudly at her and, very frightened, Biddy ran away.

Running across the field she pushed through the tall grass,
then stopped suddenly. She had nearly fallen
into a pond! Swimming on the pond were two ducks with seven ducklings

Biddy wanted to watch the ducklings, but the father duck quacked loudly at her to go away.
The mother duck swam off with all the ducklings close beside her.

Still Biddy had not found a hare. Perhaps she would find one in the wood. Going along the path, she saw a hedgehog. When she sniffed him, he rolled into a ball, and she pricked her nose on him!

The wood was a very busy place. Playing in the brambles was a baby squirrel. When the mother squirrel saw Biddy coming, she ran up a tree trunk, calling to her baby to follow her.

Tap, tap, tap, tap. What was that noise? Looking up, Biddy saw a green woodpecker. He was digging a hole in the tree trunk trying to find insects for his tea.

Among the roots of this big tree, there was a hole. As Biddy sniffed round it, a wood mouse ran out. It hurried away up the path among the bluebells.

Biddy followed the mouse along the path. At the edge of the wood was some bracken, and looking at her over the top was.... yes, it really was a HARE!

With an excited bark, Biddy was off. The hare ran very fast up the path.
With a flash of its white tail,
it disappeared through a hole in the hedge. Biddy followed it through the hedge and....

Splosh! Ugh! She was up to her neck in a big muddy puddle.
That would teach Biddy not to chase hares.

Biddy crawled out of the puddle feeling very sorry for herself. She was wet, cold and so tired. She was lost and a long way from home. She sat down and howled.

Suddenly she heard John whistling and calling her. There he was coming down the path! Happily she ran to meet him. When he saw how wet she was, John wrapped her in his pullover.

Picking her up in his arms, John hugged her. Then he told her what a naughty puppy she was to run away and get lost. Still scolding her, John carried her all the way home.

"You are so dirty," you must be bathed," John told Biddy. He put her in a bath and washed her with soap and a sponge.
Biddy hated it. She would not fall in a muddy puddle again.

When she had been dried with a soft towel, John fed her. He put her dish on the floor filled with lots of lovely meat, and Biddy forgot all about her horrible bath.

Clean, dry and very full, Biddy climbed into her basket. Oh, she was so tired after all her adventures! She scratched up her warm, blue blanket, then, curling herself into a ball, she went fast asleep.